MEL BAY PRESENTS

Open Tuning Guitar Chords

POCKETBOOK DELUXE SERIES

b

GW00771408

1

© 2006 BY MEL BAY PUBLICATIONS, INC., PACIFIC, MO 63069.
ALL RIGHTS RESERVED. INTERNATIONAL COPYRIGHT SECURED. B.M.I.
MADE AND PRINTED IN U.S.A.
No part of this publication may be reproduced in whole or in part, or stored in a retrieval
system, or transmitted in any form or by any means, electronic, mechanical, photocopy,
recording, or otherwise, without written permission of the publisher.
Visit us on the Web at www.melbay.com — E-mail us at email@melbay.com

Table of Contents

Dropped D

Tuning : **D A D G B E**
Strings : ⑥ ⑤ ④ ③ ② ①

D

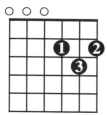

Dm

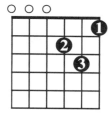

Dropped D

D7

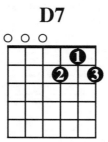

DMa7

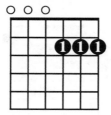

Dropped D

DMa6

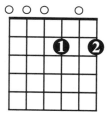

Dm6

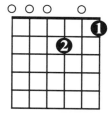

Dropped D

Dm7

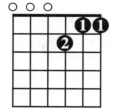

Dm-Ma7

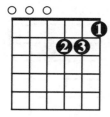

Dropped D

Dadd9

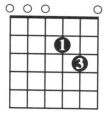

Dmadd9

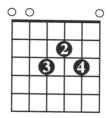

Dropped D

Dsus

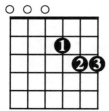

DMa7add6

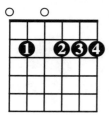

Dropped D

DMa9

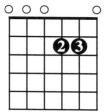

DMa13

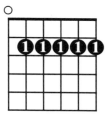

Dropped D

D69

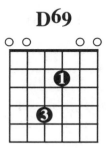

D°

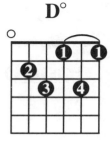

Dropped D

Em

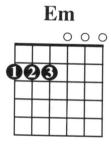

Em7

Dropped D

Fm

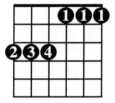

Fm7

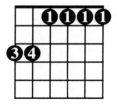

Dropped D

G

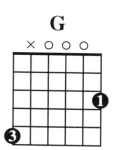

GMa7

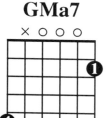

GMa6

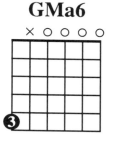

Dropped D

Gm7

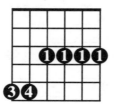

G6⁹

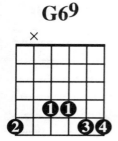

GMa9

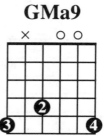

D A D G A D

Tuning : **D A D G A D**
Strings : ⑥ ⑤ ④ ③ ② ①

D

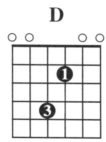

Dm

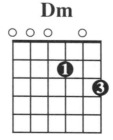

D A D G A D

D7

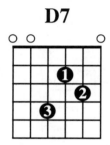

DMa7

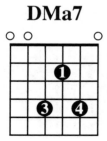

DADGAD

DMa6

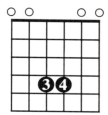

Dm6

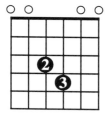

DADGAD

Dm7

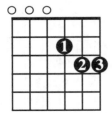

Dm-Ma7

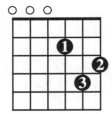

Dadd9

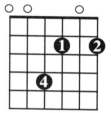

Dmadd9

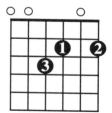

DADGAD

Dsus

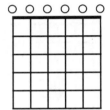

DMa7 add6

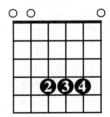

DMa9

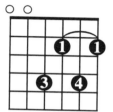

DMa13

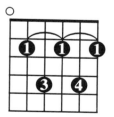

DADGAD

D69

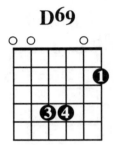

D°

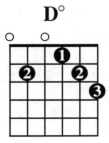

DADGAD

Em

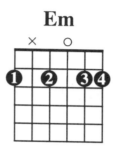

Em7

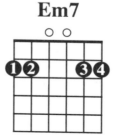

DADGAD

Fm

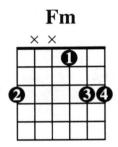

Fm7

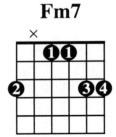

G

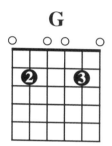

GMa7

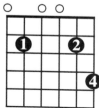

GMa6

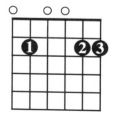

DADGAD

A

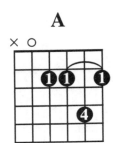

A7

Am7

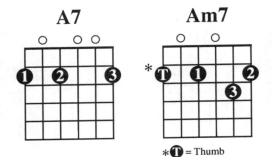

*T = Thumb

Open G

Tuning : **D G D G B D**
Strings : ⑥ ⑤ ④ ③ ② ①

G

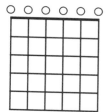

Gm

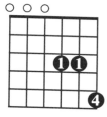

Open G

G7

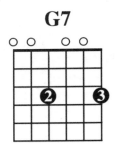

GMa7

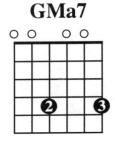

Open G

GMa6

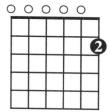

Gm6

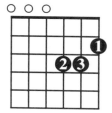

Open G

Gm7

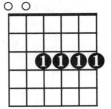

Gm-Ma7

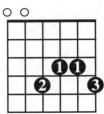

Open G

Gadd9

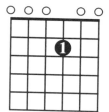

Gm add9

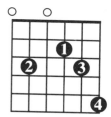

Open G

Gsus

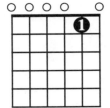

GMa7add6

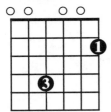

Open G

GMa9

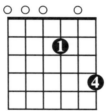

GMa13

Open G

G69

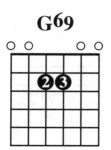

G°

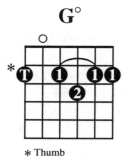

* Thumb

Open G

Am

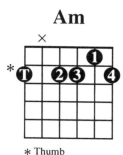

* Thumb

Am7

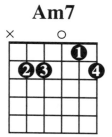

Open G

Bm

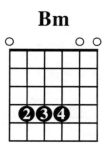

Bm7

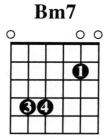

Open G

C

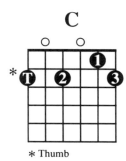

* Thumb

CMa7

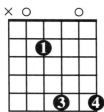

CMa6

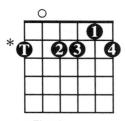

* Thumb

Open G

D

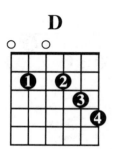

D7   Dm7

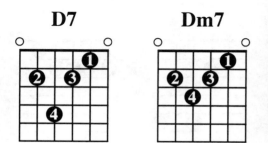

Open E

Tuning : **E B E G# B E**
Strings : **⑥ ⑤ ④ ③ ② ①**

E

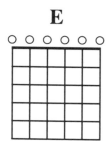

Em

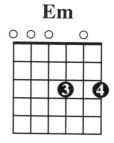

Open E

E7

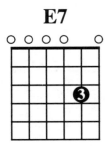

EMa7

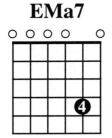

Open E

EMa6

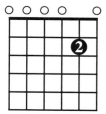

Em6

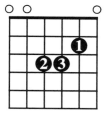

Open E

Em7

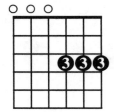

Em-Ma7

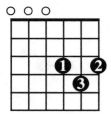

Open E

Eadd9

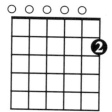

Em add9

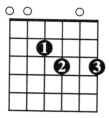

Open E

Esus

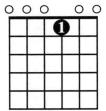

EMa7add6

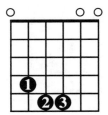

Open E

EMa9

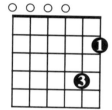

EMa13

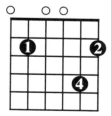

Open E

E69

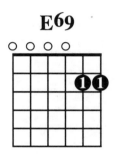

E+

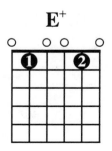

Open E

F#m

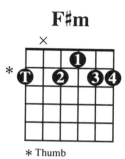

* Thumb

F#m7

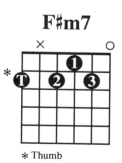

* Thumb

Open E

G#m

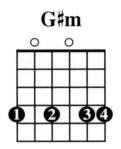

G#m7

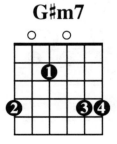

Open E

A

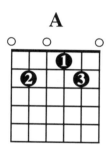

AMa7

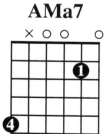

AMa6

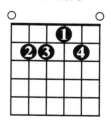

Open E

B

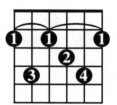

B7

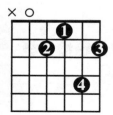

Bm7

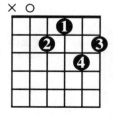

Open A

Tuning : **E A C♯ E A E**
Strings : ⑥ ⑤ ④ ③ ② ①

A

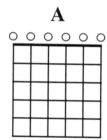

Am

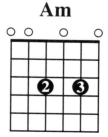

Open A

A7

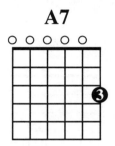

AMa7

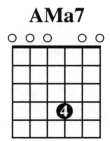

Open A

A6

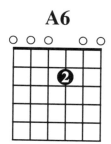

Am6

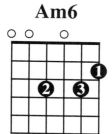

Open A

Am7

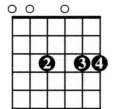

Am-Ma7

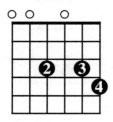

Open A

Aadd9

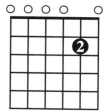

Asus

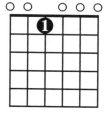

Open A

Asus

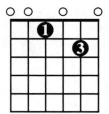

AMa7add6

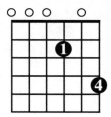

Open A

AMa9

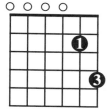

AMa13

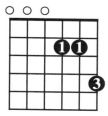

Open A

A69

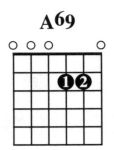

A⁺

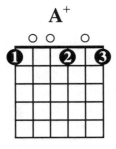

Open A

Bm

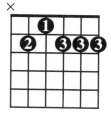

Bm7

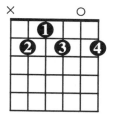

Open A

C#m

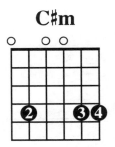

C#m7

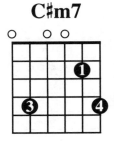

Open A

D

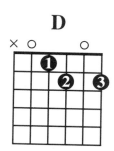

DMa7   ### DMa6

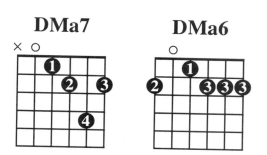

Open A

E

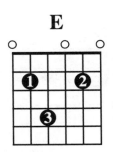

E7

Em7

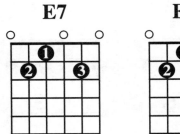

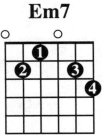

Open D

Tuning : **D A D F# A D**
Strings : ⑥ ⑤ ④ ③ ② ①

D

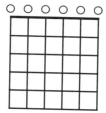

Dm

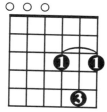

Open D

D7

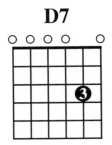

DMa7

Open D

D6

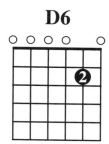

Dm6

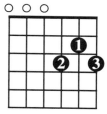

Open D

Dm7

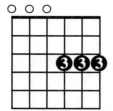

Dm-Ma7

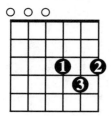

Open D

Dadd9

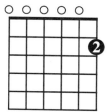

Dsus

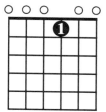

Open D

Dm add9

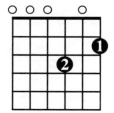

DMa7add6

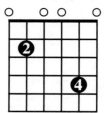

DMa9

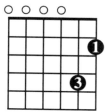

DMa13

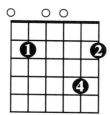

Open D

D69

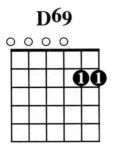

D+

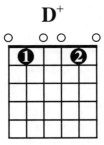

Open D

Em

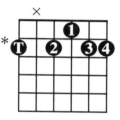

* Thumb

Em7

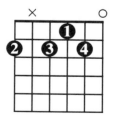

Open D

F#m

F#m7

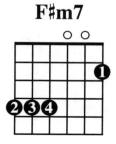

Open D

G

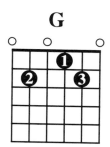

GMa7

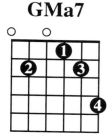

GMa6

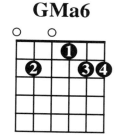

Open D

A

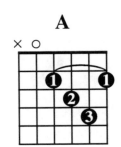

A7　　　　　　　　Am7

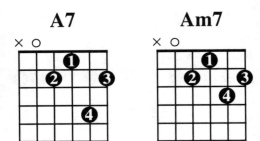

Open C

Tuning : **C G C G C E**
Strings : ⑥ ⑤ ④ ③ ② ①

C

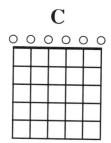

Cm

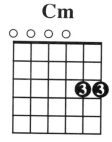

Open C

C7

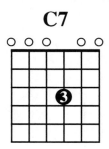

CMa7

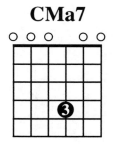

CMa6

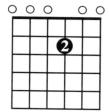

Cm6

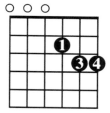

Open C

Cm7

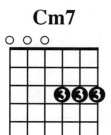

Cm-Ma7

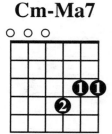

Cadd9

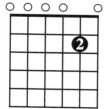

Cm add9

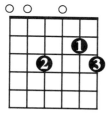

Open C

Csus

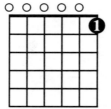

CMa7add6

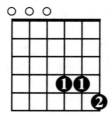

Open C

CMa9

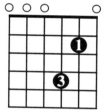

CMa13

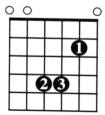

Open C

C69

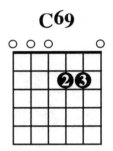

C⁺

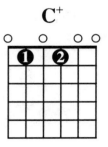

Open C

Dm

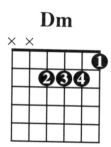

Dm7

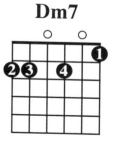

Open C

Em

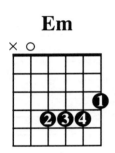

Em7

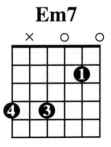

F

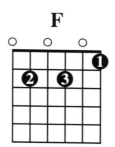

FMa7

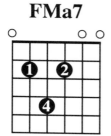

F6

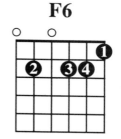

Open C

G

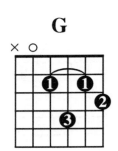

G7

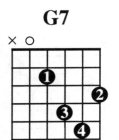

Gm7

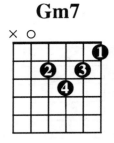

C G D G C D
"ORKNEY"

Tuning : C G D G C D
Strings : ⑥ ⑤ ④ ③ ② ①

C

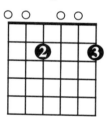

Cm

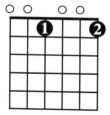

ORKNEY

C7

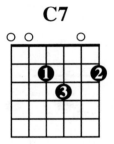

CMa7

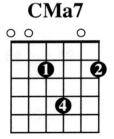

ORKNEY

C6

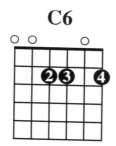

Cm6

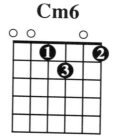

ORKNEY

Cm7

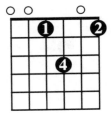

Cm-Ma7

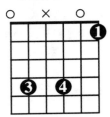

ORKNEY

Cadd9

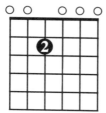

Cm add9

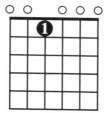

ORKNEY

Csus

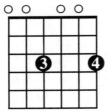

CMa7add6

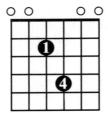

ORKNEY

C69

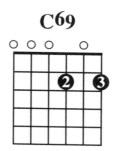

C⁺

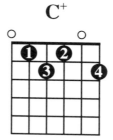

ORKNEY

Dm

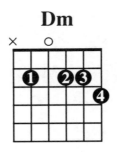

Dm7

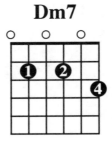

ORKNEY

F

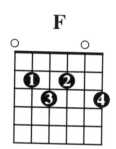

FMa7

FMa6

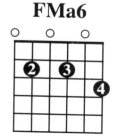

ORKNEY

G

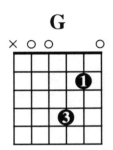

G7

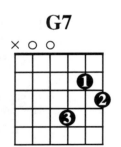

Gm7

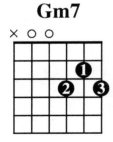